Dear mouse friends,
Welcome to the world of

Geronimo Stilton

Geronimo Stilton
A learned and brainy
mouse; editor of
The Rodent's Gazette

Thea Stilton
Geronimo's sister and
special correspondent at
The Rodent's Gazette

Trap Stilton
An awful joker;
Geronimo's cousin and
owner of the store
Cheap Junk for Less

Benjamin Stilton
A sweet and loving
nine-year-old mouse;
Geronimo's favorite
nephew

Geronimo Stilton

THIS HOTEL IS HAUNTED!

Scholastic Inc.

New York   Toronto   London   Auckland

Sydney   Mexico City   New Delhi   Hong Kong

ISBN 978-0-545-34102-8

Based on an original idea by Elisabetta Dami.
www.geronimostilton.com

Published by Scholastic Inc., 557 Broadway, New York, NY 10012.
SCHOLASTIC and associated logos are trademarks and/or registered trademarks of Scholastic Inc.

Stilton is the name of a famous English cheese. It is a registered trademark of the Stilton Cheese Makers' Association. For more information, go to www.stiltoncheese.com.

Text by Geronimo Stilton
Original title *Lo strano caso del Fantasma al Grand Hotel*
Cover by Giuseppe Ferrario
Illustrations by Valeria Turati
Graphics by Michela Battaglin

Special thanks to Beth Dunfey
Translated by Julia Heim
Interior design by Kay Petronio

12 11 10 9 8 7 6 5 4 3 2 1   12 13 14 15 16 17/0

40

Printed in the U.S.A.
First printing, July 2012

A MYSTERIOUS GHOST STORY

Dear mouse friends, my name is Stilton, *Geronimo Stilton*. I am the editor of *The Rodent's Gazette*, the most **FAMOUSE** newspaper on Mouse Island. I'm also a writer by trade, and I love books.

I'm **glad** you're reading — I have a thrilling new **STORY** to tell!

It all started one morning while I was having **breakfast**. As I **poured** a cup of piping-**HOT** tea, I turned on the television.

THE RODENT'S GAZETTE

The **NEWSMOUSE Pippi Skinnyfur** announced, "Late-breaking news! We are here at *New Mouse City's Grand Hotel*, where all the guests are leaving because of a GHOST!"

AS I WAS HAVING BREAKFAST . . .

A ghost? I almost dropped my teacup. Had I heard right? Had she really said a GHOST?

"Yes, that's right, you heard me, a GHOST!" Ms. Skinnyfur continued.

. . . I TURNED ON THE TV AND STARED.

"How **strange**!" I exclaimed. "Every mouse knows there's no such thing as ghosts!"

Behind Ms. Skinnyfur, rodents were scurrying out of the hotel. I could hear them squeaking, "We want our money back!"

A GHOST AT THE GRAND HOTEL?!

Ms. Skinnyfur began interviewing the

owner of the Grand Hotel, **Horatzio Hoteltail**. "Mr. Hoteltail, a CREEPY ghost has been HAUNTING your hotel for about a month now. Is there anything you want to say to your guests?"

Poor Horatzio had tears in his eyes. "I want to extend a very sincere apology to our guests! I will refund all their **money**."

"What will become of the Grand Hotel? It's one of New Mouse City's most beloved institutions. Will it be forced to CLOSE?" Ms. Skinnyfur asked.

I turned off the television. The whole situation was STRANGE.

I was concerned about poor Horatzio. He was an old friend of mine. Back in elemousery school, we used to spend our afternoons scampering around his family's hotel.

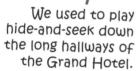

When we were young mice, my friend Hercule Poirat and I always did our home-work at Horatzio's.

We used to play hide-and-seek down the long hallways of the Grand Hotel.

Then we would have a snack in the hotel's enormouse kitchens . . .

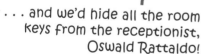

. . . and we'd hide all the room keys from the receptionist, Oswald Rattaldo!

WHO? WHAT? WHEN? WHERE? WHY?

When I left the house, I found a surprise waiting for me. On the doormat there was a letter addressed to me, *Geronimo Stilton*.

I was overcome with **curiosity**. I turned the package over and found a card that said:

Geronimo Stilton
8 Mouseford Lane
New Mouse City,
Mouse Island 13131

Go immediately to

THE GRAND HOTEL.

Room number 313 has been reserved for you. Wait for me there. But do not squeak of this letter to anyone (anyone at all)!

GERONIMO'S HOUSE
8 MOUSEFORD LANE

GRAND HOTEL
3 MOZZARELLA WAY

Perplexed, I put the letter back into its envelope. A million questions scampered through my mind.

WHO was inviting me to the Grand Hotel?

WHAT did the sender want from me?

WHEN had the mysterious invitation been sent?

WHERE had it come from?

And above all . . . **WHY**?

I was torn. I was **INTRIGUED** by the letter, but I was also **AFRAID** of ghosts!

Eventually, curiosity won out. So I called a taxi to take me to the Grand Hotel.

When we arrived, a **bellhop** opened the door. "Welcome to *NEW MOUSE CITY'S GRAND HOTEL*!" he declared. His squeak sounded confident, but his whiskers were twitching nervously.

There was a crowd of rodents leaving the hotel. I was the only one who wanted to go in!

A mouse in her bathrobe ran out the door, SCREAMING, "I can't stay here a second longer!"

I pushed through the revolving door and found myself in the LOBBY. The last of the guests were departing.

BELLHOP

At large hotels, there is always a uniformed bellhop at the door. He greets guests as they arrive and calls taxis for guests who are leaving.

LOBBY

The lobby is the hotel's indoor entrance area. In large hotels, it is a very spacious and elegant room where you can find the reception and checkout desks and the café.

1 - MAIN ENTRANCE
2 - CHECK-IN
3 - INFORMATION
4 - CHECKOUT
5 - RESERVATIONS
6 - ELEVATORS
7 - CAFÉ

ROOM 313

I approached the **reception** desk, where Oswald Rattaldo, the receptionist, was seated. I noticed that his eyes were red, as if he had been crying.

A guest scurried past, *yelling*, "We want a full refund, do you hear me? I'd rather spend the night in a cat clinic than stay in this hotel another minute!"

"I'm sorry, sir, we have never had a GHOST at the Grand Hotel before!" Oswald sighed.

"Good morning, Oswald,

RECEPTION

The reception desk is in the lobby. It's where guest check in and receive their room keys. When it's time to leave, guests come here to check out and ask for the bill.

how are you?" I said. "I'm here for room 313."

Oswald recognized me immediately. "Mr. Geronimo! What a pleasure to see you again!" he said happily. "I see that Suite 313 has been reserved in your name. Come, I will take you upstairs right away."

Entering room 313 was like going back in time. Even though it had been years since I'd been inside the hotel, I remembered the canopy bed, the cheddar-colored carpet, and the golden cheese slice wallpaper.

I thanked Oswald for bringing me up. Then I went into the bathroom to wash my paws. Even the bathroom had remained the same. The only new detail I saw was the shower curtain, which was decorated with a pattern of bananas.

SUITE

Suite is a French word (pronounced sweet) that means "series of rooms" or "apartment." A suite is usually made up of a bedroom, a bathroom, and a small living room.

I frowned. That was a bit odd. **Bananas**?

That was when I heard a soft voice **squeaking** my name. "Geronimoooo . . ."

I gulped. Could it be the **GHOST**? No, it was probably just my overactive imagination.

I leaned over to turn on the tap. That was when I heard it again.

"Geronimoooo . . ."

Strange!

I picked up the paw towel. Again I heard, "Geronimoooo . . ."

Very strange!

Suddenly, the shower curtain began moving. Something inside it was reaching toward me! Its arms were open wide, like the tentacles of an octopus.

I was so **scared**, I could barely open my snout to squeak, "**HEEEELLLLLLLP!**"

That was when a tail popped out from behind the curtain, then a paw, and finally a rat's snout. "**Peekaboo!**"

I jumped backward. "Wh-wh-who is it?"

A mouse with gray fur and WHISKERS shiny with fur gel poked his snout out.

"My dear Stilton, how did you like my little joke?" he asked, smirking.

Only then did I recognize him. It was my friend **Hercule Poirat**! He's a detective, and loves mysteries the way mice love cheese.

Unfortunately for me, he also *loves* playing jokes. And I'm his favorite target! (It's not my fault I'm a 'fraidy mouse.)

I should've realized something was up when I saw that banana-patterned shower curtain. Hercule just **loves** bananas . . . and he knows how much I **detest** them!

STRANGE THINGS ARE HAPPENING AT THE GRAND HOTEL!

"What are you doing here, Hercule?" I demanded.

"**Strange** things are happening at the Grand Hotel," he replied seriously. "Scrape the **cheese** out of your ears, Stilton! Even a scaredy-rat like you knows that GHOSTS don't exist. So who has been TERRORIZING the guests at this hotel for the last month?"

Then he lowered his squeak. "I need your help to find out!"

I sighed. "Hercule, you know that I'm a very busy mouse. I have a new book to write, and —"

"I'm begging you, my dear Stilton!"

Hercule cried. "If you don't want to do it for me, do it for our city! The GRAND HOTEL is a beloved New Mouse City establishment, and that is precious. Think about how many rodents work at the GRAND HOTEL. You don't want them to lose their jobs, do you? Plus, we simply must help our old friend Horatzio! He needs us."

Then he lit up. "I have a GENIUS IDEA! Let's go to him now! He will convince you!"

Before I could protest, he was dragging me to Horatzio's office.

Heeeellllllp!

A GREAT LOVE STORY!

We found Horatzio at his desk, sobbing. "Oh, my dear friends, whatever will I do? I'll be forced to sell my hotel! For generations this hotel has belonged to my family. **Ahh, what a cat-astrophe!**"

"Come on, Horatzio, take a tissue." Hercule consoled him. "**HAVE NO FEAR**, Hercule Poirat is here! Your old friend Geronimo and I will **HELP** you. Please calm down.

We need to ask you some questions."

Horatzio brightened up at once. "Really? You'll really help me?"

I sighed. You see, I truly am a busy mouse. I have stories to edit and deadlines to meet and a newspaper to put out. But I simply can't refuse a **FRIEND** in need!

I took out a notebook and began jotting down some notes. "Tell us everything, starting from the beginning."

Horatzio *pointed* at a painting behind his desk. It depicted a CURLY-WHISKERED rodent and an elegant, *smiling* female rodent.

EVEREST AND
ARABELLA HOTELTAIL

"Do you remember these mice, Geronimo? They are my great-grandparents

EVEREST AT WORK

Everest and **Arabella Hoteltail**. They were the ones who founded the New Mouse City Grand Hotel years and years ago. Theirs was a great love story — oh, how they loved each other!

"My great-grandfather was a **bricklayer**, and my great-grandmother was a **cook**. They were poor, but full of energy and enthusiasm. Everest decided to build a hotel, brick by brick. And guests came from all over Mouse Island to **taste** Arabella's delicious dishes."

Horatzio took a deep breath and then went

ARABELLA IN THE KITCHEN

on. "My great-grandparents loved making travelers happy. Inviting them to enjoy **hot** meals and **comfortable** beds was their life's work!

"Over the years, the hotel got bigger. It became the most **FAMOUSE** hotel in the city, and then on all of Mouse Island. But now this **GHOST** is **ruining** me! Soon I will be forced to sell the hotel to that awful rodent. . . ."

My ears perked up. "Someone wants you

THE GRAND HOTEL BACK IN THE TIME OF HORATZIO'S GREAT-GRANDPARENTS

to sell the hotel? **Who?**"

"A mysterious businessmouse, **BRADLEY BIGBOTTOM**. For the last month, he has been asking me to sell it to him at a **really, really low** price. And now it seems I have no choice, with this **GHOST** wandering the halls for the past month. All the guests have been complaining and fleeing the hotel! And do you know what that **slimy sewer rat** wants to do to my hotel? He wants to turn it into . . .

Hercule was outraged. "A toilet factory? **Never!** They'll have to flush us out of here first! Isn't that right, my dear Stilton? Did you get my little joke? **FLUSH** us out of here . . . get it?"

I just rolled my eyes. I was too busy thinking about what Horatzio had said to laugh at Hercule's silly pun. For a **MONTH** a **MYSTERiOUS RODENT** had been asking Horatzio to sell. . . . For a **MONTH** a ghost had wandered around the hotel. . . . For a **MONTH** all the guests had complained.

A month?

A month?

A month?

THE SECRETS OF THE GRAND HOTEL

I turned to Horatzio. "Please show us where, how, and when this GHOST appears!"

Horatzio nodded and picked up a set of **KEYS**. "I'll take you on a tour of the whole hotel while we talk."

As he led us down a hallway, he continued with his **tale**. "Many mice have seen GHOST here. The first ones to complain were guests who come to our hotel regularly, Count and Countess Von Ratsis. They were returning to their room after a reception

Count and Countess Von Ratsis

at Countess de Snobberella's castle when they found themselves snout-to-snout with the ghost!"

"**Blistering bananas!** I guess this ghost doesn't appear for just any old rat," Hercule exclaimed.

"Then he scared the entire **Rodentine family**," Horatzio went on. "Those poor mice! Oswald saw them leave in a hurry, with looks of horror frozen onto their snouts. Then, a few days later, two **elderly mice**

The Rodentine family

saw the ghost while they were getting out of the elevator. . . ."

As Horatzio continued his tale, we toured the *GRAND HOTEL* from the basement to the attic. It was huge!

WHO SAW THE GHOST?

Finally, we came back to the lobby. "We would like to talk to all the ladies and gentlemice who work at the *GRAND HOTEL*," Hercule announced. Horatzio answered sadly, "Please feel free to interview them — the ones who remain, that is. Many of our employees have also been SCARED AWAY by the ghost."

At the entrance to the hotel, we found **Oswald** again. "What a shame to lose this **precious** landmark, Mr. Geronimo," he said gravely. "The

Oswald Rattaldo

Grand Hotel is the heart of our city."

"We will do everything we can to help Horatzio," I assured him. "But tell me, have you seen the GHOST?"

Oswald shook his snout. "No, he never passed by me. But many guests have described him to me — they say he GLOWS in the dark!"

I jotted down what he'd said in my notebook: GLOWS IN THE DARK.

Next we went to look for the hotel's housekeeper, **MATILDA BROOMMOUSE**. We checked in housekeeping headquarters, but we didn't see her anywhere — until we heard someone sobbing in the broom closet.

Matilda Broommouse

I kissed her paw in greeting. (I am a real *gentlemouse*!) "Good day, Miss Broommouse. Why are you crying?"

"I—I—I don't want to lose my job," she stammered.

"Do not worry, **Miss Broommouse**, we are on the case!" Hercule assured her. "Tell me, have you seen the ghost? When? And what were you doing?"

She sobbed. "I saw him coming down the stairs. . . . *Sigh* . . . He scared all the guests away!" Then she screamed, "Look! Another spiderweb! Since the ghost has been here, I keep finding them all over, even if I dust every day. I do a good job, please tell **HORATZIO** that! It's not my fault the guests keep running away."

"Calm down, dear Miss Broommouse, the

hotel is in good paws! We will **save** it," Hercule responded.

In my notebook I wrote: **spiderwebs**.

Next we went to see the hotel's cook, **Sergio Creampuff**. We found him in the kitchen, seated in front of the stove. "Who would have thought that the Grand Hotel would *close* after so many years?" he sighed.

"Have you ever seen the GHOST?" I asked.

"Yes, every time a guest saw the ghost, it

Sergio Creampuff

would also **appear** in the kitchen. It was big and tall, with creepy clanking armor and chains."

"I see. Have you noticed anything else **strange**?" I asked. "I mean, besides the fact that there seems to be a ghost."

The cook pulled on his whiskers thoughtfully. "Weeeelll, there *is* something, now that you mention it. For a month now, all the guests have been complaining about finding WHITE FUR in their soup. But no one here in the kitchen has white fur! Also, I keep finding **chocolate wrappers** on the floor, but no one in the kitchen eats chocolates."

I jotted down
big, tall, chains, white fur, chocolate wrappers.

We said good-bye to Sergio and went to the hotel's basement to look for the electrician,

Jack Joltson

Jack Joltson. We found him changing a lightbulb.

Hercule and I introduced ourselves. Jack was very happy that someone was investigating the strange situation at the _GRAND HOTEL_.

"Have you see the ghost or noticed anything **STRANGE** since the GHOST first appeared?" I asked him.

"I haven't seen the ghost," Jack said. "But there is one thing I don't understand. Ever since the hotel started being haunted, I keep hearing eerie **violin** music. But the hotel isn't wired with a stereo system!"

I nodded and jotted what he'd

said in my notebook: violin music.

Hercule winked. "This ghost is BRAINIER than a lab rat! But it's only a matter of time before we unmask him, right, my dear Stilton?"

Next we needed to find Casey Valise, the head bellhop. But there weren't any more guests around for him to help, and no one knew where he had gone.

We decided to go back to see Oswald. We found Casey keeping him company at the reception desk.

Casey lit up when he saw us. "Can I carry a bag for you, sir?"

I smiled warmly. "No thank you, Casey. But I would like to ask you a question. Have you seen the GHOST?"

 Casey pulled out a bright plastic ring and began to fiddle with

CASEY VALISE

it. "I'm not sure I've seen him. But I did find this one evening. Do you think it might be a **clue**?"

As I reached out to take it, I noticed that it was GLOWING. Hmm . . . could it belong to the ghost?

I jotted down: plastic ring, glows in the dark.

Finally, we went to the Grand Hotel's main office to meet the hotel's director, **MS. Bertha**. We entered a very elegant room that smelled of expensive perfume. I knew the scent quite well — it was the same one worn by my arch-nemesis, Sally Ratmousen, the director of *The Daily Rat*. That **odor**

Ms. Bertha

was enough to send a shiver down my tail.

The room was filled with *precious objects*: embroidered silk pillows, antique furniture, paintings by famouse artists.

Ms. Bertha was standing at her desk. She was **TALL** and a bit **stout** and dressed beautifully in a very elegant black suit. Her paws GLITTERED with jewelry.

Ms. Bertha looked at us and Sighed. "Oh, I am so sorry that the Grand Hotel has to close!" I also heard her mumble under her breath, "Nothing lasts forever!"

"And what will you do when the Grand Hotel closes, Ms. Bertha?" I asked her.

"Oh, a manager like me will have options,

of course," she said **proudly**. "Why, I've already been offered a position as director of the toilet factory . . . um, I mean, I will certainly find another job. With my experience, I won't have any trouble! But now, please excuse me. I must get back to work. There is so much to do these days!"

So Hercule and I left her office and went looking for **HORATZIO**. We wanted to fill him in on everything we'd learned from his employees.

We found him in the **elevator**, and together we returned to room 313. As Hercule slid the key into the lock, he commented, "It was quite interesting to listen to everyone's stories, wasn't it, my dear Stilton? Let's review our notes all together and see if we can deduce anything!"

A Genius Idea!

As we entered the suite, Hercule exclaimed, "I have a genius idea! Tonight we will sleep here! Alone! And we will give that ghost the **SURPRISE** of his life (or death, as the case might be)! What do you think, my dear Stilton? Isn't that a genius idea?"

I'll be honest with you, dear reader. I thought it was a *terrible* idea! As you know, I'm quite a 'fraidy mouse. The last thing I wanted was to spend the night in a **HAUNTED** hotel.

"Umm, **SLEEP** here tonight?" I mumbled. "To surprise the GHOST?

What if *he's* the one to surprise *us*?"

"Maybe it would be **SAFER** if I stayed here, too," Horatzio proposed.

"My dear Horatzio, that is very kind of you, but it is totally unnecessary! We aren't **AFRAID**!" Hercule replied. "Are we, Stilton?"

"N-n-nooo, I-I'm not s-s-scared," I stammered. "But if Horatzio insists —"

Hercule cut me off. "It's okay, Horatzio. Why don't you leave us to our work now? Oh, but before you go, I would like to get some room service. Here's my order:

1 large bunch of bananas!
1 banana-flavored fondue!
5 banana cream pies!
6 banana splits!
8 pounds of candied bananas!
10 jars of banana jam!

4 large pizzas with bananas on top!
4 extra-large banana smoothies!
10 banana-nut muffins!
5 boxes of banana-flavored chocolates!"

"You see, solving mysteries always makes me hungry, and my brain works better when my stomach is full . . . of bananas! Hmm, better make it *two* bunches of bananas — no, how about *three*? You never know when you might need a little extra BRAIN power!" Hercule exclaimed. "We're going to stay up all **night**, listening for the ghost to howl, '*Ooooooooooooh. . . .*'"

I shivered. "The ghost howls?"

"I don't know if it howls, but it sounded SPOOKY, didn't it?" Hercule snickered. "My dear Stilton, you should see how pALe you've gotten. Is something bothering you?"

"Pale? I'm pale all right!" I shrieked.

"I CAN'T TAKE IT ANYMORE! I'm out of here!"

"Please stay, Geronimo!" Horatzio begged me as he left. "If you and Hercule don't solve this mystery, I'm **ruined**!"

Soon, Horatzio returned with waiters bringing all the food **Hercule** had ordered. As soon as Hercule had his paws on the bananas, he tossed Horatzio and the waiters out like yesterday's cheese rinds. "**SHOO!** Everyone out now! Let me work!"

Then he hung a sign on the door:

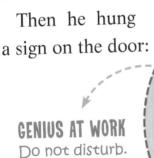

GENIUS AT WORK
Do not disturb.

A GHASTLY NIGHT . . .

As soon as everyone was gone, Hercule lit two candles, turned off the lights, and whispered, "And now, we wait."

"Wait for what?" I whispered back.

"Wait for the ghost to show his snout!" Hercule hissed.

"Maybe he won't come . . . ," I whispered hopefully.

"Noooo, I'm certain he'll appear," Hercule hissed.

Ummm...

"Why did you light candles instead of turning on the light?" I whispered.

"Candles add a bit of mystery. You like mysteries, don't you, my dear Stilton?" he whispered.

"No, I do not like mysteries!" I whispered vehemently. "You know very well that I am a complete scaredy-mouse! Why are we whispering?"

"Because in plaaaaces where there are ghooooosts, one should never squeak loooooooudly . . . ," Hercule whispered. His squeak was quite creepy.

That was it. I lost my cheese. "I CAN'T TAKE IT ANYMORE!" I shouted.

Hercule just looked at me sympathetically. You really are quite a scaredy-mouse."

At that moment, the door burst open. . . .

"Aaaaaaack!" I screamed in terror. "It's

THE GHOOOOOOOOOOOOOOOOOOST!"

But it was only Horatzio. "Sorry, friends, I didn't mean to **scare** you! I just wanted to warn you that the phone lines have **Suddenly** gone down."

I was so **embarrassed**. "Oh, yes . . . um . . . I — I was just doing some *tests* so we'd be ready when the GHOST appears . . . ," I stammered.

"Ha ha ha!" Hercule laughed. "You were testing your **SCREAM** of terror!"

"Good night, my friends!" Horatzio said.

I **sighed**. I had a sinking feeling that the night would be **ghastly**!

Ha ha ha!

IIIIIII'M THE
GHOOOOOST. . . .

Hercule plopped onto the bed and **sank** into the feather pillows. Then he opened the mini-fridge with the tip of his tail and took out a **cheese soda**. With one paw, he sampled a banana-flavored chocolate, and with the other he turned on the **TV**.

"Look on the bright side, my dear Stilton. Here we are in the most *luxurious* hotel in all of New Mouse City . . . for free! We've got silk sheets, *feathery* pillows, a mini-fridge

filled with the finest cheesy beverages and snacks, plus all the TV stations you could ever want! It's positively banana-rific!"

I shivered. "Unfortunately, the service also includes a GHOST!"

"Pshaw!" Hercule scoffed. "This ghost is nothing a whisker-licking-good **investigator** like me can't handle!"

I sighed. As usual, Hercule had strong-pawed me into doing exactly what he wanted.

I bent down to get a bottle of water from the fridge. That was when someone WHISPERED into my ear, "IIIII'm the ghoooooost. . . ."

H-help!

I nearly **JUMPED** out of my fur. "Who said that? H-help!"

It was Hercule. "Did you like my little joke? Hee hee hee!

Scaring you is easier than taking a banana from a baby mouseling!"

That was the last slice of cheese, as far as I was concerned. "I CAN'T TAKE IT ANYMORE!" I shrieked.

I scampered into the bathroom, but as soon as I went in, the lights clicked off. Someone howled, "IIIIII'm the ghooooooooost. . . ."

"Wh-who is that?" I squeaked. "H-help!"

It was Hercule, of course. He turned the lights back on. He was rolling on the floor, laughing. "Hee hee hee, you should see yourself, Stilton! Your tail is all twisted up from FRIGHT!"

H-help!

Exasperated, I went out onto the balcony to get some air. But the curtain behind me shook as a ghostly voice HOWLED, "Ooooooh, did you thiiiiink

HEELLLP!

you could hiiiiiide?"

"HEEELLLLLLP!"

I screamed in terror.

Naturally, it was Hercule again. "You can't even tell the difference between a curtain and a ghost, can you, my dear Stilton?" He **snickered**. "Hmph, you're so easy to scare, it's no fun playing pranks on you!"

At that moment, the lights went out!

"Enough with the tricks, Hercule!" I screamed. "Turn the lights back on!"

"B-b-but I didn't turn them off!" he stammered.

"Stop playing around, Poirat!"

"I-I-I'm telling you I didn't turn off the light!" Hercule exclaimed.

The blood **FROZE** in my veins. "Well, if you didn't, *then who did*?"

THEN WHO DID? THEN WHO DID?

THEN WHO DID?

THEN WHO DID?

THEN WHO DID?

THEN WHO DID?

THEN WHO DID?

THEN WHO DID?

THEN WHO DID?

THEN WHO DID?

THEN WHO DID? THEN WHO DID?

Do You Think That Was the Ghost?

A key turned in the lock, and the door to our suite burst open.

A spine-chilling squeak howled, "It was meeeeee . . . THE GHOOOOOOST!"

Hercule and I were so terrified we screeched:

"HEEEEEEEELLLLLLLLLLLLLLLP!"
"HEEEEEEEEELLLLLLLLLLLLLLLP!"

In the dark, we saw a GLOWING ghostly figure dressed in heavy **armor** draped with **SpiDeRWebs**. Thick **white fur** poked out from under his helmet.

The ghost was dragging long, glowing chains behind him . . . but they didn't make any noise! Instead, I heard *violin music*

that seemed to come from far away. It was a creepy tune that sent a chill down my tail.

The ghost waved its chains in the air and howled, "GEEEEEEETTTTT OUT OF HEEEEERE, ALLLLL OF YOOOUUUU! THIS IS MYYYYYYYY HOTELLLLL. GEEEEEETTTT OUUUUUUUT!"

Then he gave a gloomy cackle and left, slamming the door behind him.

A moment later, the LIGHTS clicked back on. I took a deeeeeeeeep breath and realized . . . I was all alone! "Poirat! Hercule Poirat, where are you?"

A tiny squeak whispered from the far side of the suite: "I'm over here, my dear Stilton!"

Hercule was WHITER than mold on Brie. He scrambled out of his hiding place and peeled a banana with trembling paws.

"I'm going to need the power of potassium

to get through this!" he said. "Well, what do you think, my dear Stilton? Was that the GHOST?"

I nodded. "I was so SCARED my tail is in tangles," I muttered.

"Ohh, yes, yes . . . he was truly t-terrifying!" Hercule stammered. "I was scared myself. Please forgive me for *poking fun* at you before."

I gave him a hearty slap on the tail. "Don't worry about it! Anyone can get scared. The important thing is to try to **overcome** your fears."

Then I told him what Aunt Sweetfur always used to tell me: "Never let fear conquer your love of adventure!"

NEVER LET FEAR CONQUER YOUR LOVE OF ADVENTURE!

"'Never let fear conquer your love of adventure!'" Hercule repeated. "Burnt banana bread, your aunt is a really intelligent rodent!"

He threw out his **banana peel** and repeated, "Never let fear conquer your love of adventure! I'm not afraid of the ghost (since ghosts don't exist), and I'm not even afraid of the **DARK**! But most of all, I'm

not afraid because I'm not alone. I have a dear friend with me. And we will help each other be brave!"

With that, he grabbed a flashlight and scurried toward the door.

"Follow me, my dear Stilton. Let's reveal the **MOUSE** behind the mask! By the time we're through with him, the only place he'll be shaking his chains is in Ratcatraz Prison!"

"You said it, Poirat! I'm right behind you," I declared.

Together, we *hurried* down the dark corridor.

SOMEONE WENT THROUGH HERE . . .

In the distance, we heard a loud **BANG**.

Strange . . . There wasn't anyone at the end of the corridor!

We inspected the walls, looking for some sort of **secret passage**, but we didn't find anything that looked like a door.

"Where could the **GHOST** have gone?" I murmured, shivering. "He seems to have disappeared, almost as if he went right through the wall." I **remembered** Aunt Sweetfur's advice. "There's no such thing as **GHOSTS**. . . . There's no such thing as **GHOSTS** . . . ," I murmured, trying to reassure myself.

I was still looking for clues when suddenly

Hercule called, "Yoo-hoo! Over here! I think I've found something, my dear Stilton!"

He showed me an air-conditioning **grate** that was slightly crooked. There was a screw on the floor, as if someone had tried to put the grate back on in a *hurry*.

"Someone went through here," Hercule muttered. "And it wasn't a GHOST, or my name isn't Hercule Poirat!"

We opened the air-conditioning grate. Inside, we found **pawprints** that glowed in the dark!

"How **strange**!" I said.

FIRST CLUE!

"Yes," agreed Hercule, nodding wisely. "One doesn't usually see pawprints in air-conditioning ducts . . . especially not GLOWING pawprints!"

I remembered that the ghost had been glowing when we'd seen him. A lightbulb went off in my brain. These pawprints might be from glow-in-the-dark paint!

I told Hercule my theory. "Let's follow the prints!" he declared.

We crawled into the air-conditioning duct. It was so narrow that we had to continue on all fours. Hercule bumped into me, and I banged my snout on the top of the duct.

"Be careful now, my dear Stilton!" Hercule said, chuckling. "You don't want to damage your little gray cells, now do you?"

"They're probably already damaged — by fear. I CAN'T TAKE IT ANYMORE!" I shrieked.

Hercule pinched my tail. "My dear Stilton, you're more skittish than a kitten in a dog kennel. Calm down!"

Right then, I noticed something weird: The air-conditioning duct was full of **spiderwebs**.

SECOND CLUE!

Strange! There shouldn't be any spiderwebs in an air-conditioning duct.

I remembered something **Matilda Broommouse** had told us. She'd said that since the ghost had started appearing, she'd spotted spiderwebs all over the hotel.

We crawled along till the duct ended, and we found ourselves in the kitchen. On the floor in front of us was a pile of **chocolate wrappers**.

THIRD CLUE!

Strange! Ghosts don't eat chocolates.

But I remembered that Sergio Creampuff kept finding chocolate wrappers in the kitchen.

We followed the pawprints all the way to a door. We opened it . . . and discovered a staircase!

We followed the **tracks** up the stairs until we found ourselves in front of a little door.

Of course . . . it was the entrance to the attic! Horatzio had shown it to us during our tour.

Hercule and I exchanged glances. Then we opened the door.

It was **DARK** inside the attic, and it smelled of mold, dust, and forgotten objects. At one end there was an old canopy bed with **moth-eaten** curtains. In the corners stood worn-out, unwanted items: PAINTINGS with chipped frames, beat-up old *lamps*, moldy pillows with ripped linings. But there wasn't a soul anywhere, not even a mouse.

I reached under the bed to make sure no one was hiding there. My paw touched something with long fur.

"AAAAAAAAAAAAACK! A CAT!!!" I screamed.

I was about to faint from fright when I heard Hercule chuckling. "That's no cat! It's just a **white wig**."

FOURTH CLUE!

Strange! I had never seen a white wig around the Grand Hotel before.

Then I remembered that guests had complained to Sergio Creampuff about white fur they'd found in their soup.

I gathered my courage and continued exploring the attic. I noticed a tall wardrobe and decided to check it out. When I opened it, I found **armor**!

FIFTH CLUE!

Strange! I had never seen any armor in the hallways of the Grand Hotel.

Then I remembered the GHOST we had seen was wearing armor.

Suddenly, some **chains** that had been resting on top of the wardrobe fell onto my snout!

SIXTH CLUE!

Strange! The chains bounced right off me . . . because they were made of plastic!

Then I remembered that Casey Valise had found a plastic ring after the ghost had appeared.

Hercule and I kept searching for **CLUES**. We soon discovered an air-conditioning duct in the attic with a portable stereo inside. I pushed PLAY, and gloomy VIOLIN MUSIC filled the air.

SEVENTH CLUE!

Strange! An air-conditioning duct was an unusual place to put a portable stereo.

Then I remembered that Jack Joltson

had said he kept hearing strange music.

"Spiderwebs . . . chocolates . . . a white wig . . . armor . . . chains . . . music . . . we found it all!" Hercule declared. "Everything except the glow-in-the-dark paint."

At that moment, I accidentally stepped into a can of glowing paint. "I found that, too, Hercule!" I exclaimed.

"That does it, my dear Stilton!" Hercule declared. "This phantom is a big, fat phony! Some trickster has been dressing up as a ghost!"

"We've got to find him!" I shouted, and stroked my snout thoughtfully. "I think I know someone who might be able to HELP us."

A Little Help from a Friend

First thing the next morning, Hercule and I strolled into Tricks for Tails, a joke shop on Fastrat Lane. The owner, **PAWS PRANKSTER**, was a good friend of my cousin Trap.

"Hiya, Geronimo!" Paws shouted from the back. "How are you?"

"I'm fine," I replied. "But I'm looking for something special —"

Before I could finish squeaking, I felt something **FURRY** tickling my neck. "Heeeeellllllllp! A spider!" I screamed.

Then I realized that it was merely one of Paws's **PRANKS**. The spider was actually a rubber toy! "Funny, very funny," I muttered. "But I'd really like to talk

to you about *serious* business. . . ."

That was when I felt something **slimey** under my paw.

"Heeeellllllllp! A snake!" I yelled. Then I realized that it was another **trick**.

As Paws and Hercule giggled, I tried to continue. "I want to ask y—"

Suddenly, a **SKULL** on a shelf lit up. Its teeth chattered as it howled, "Howdy, Cheeseheads!"

"**HEEEELLLLLLLLLLLP!**"
I squealed. "A talking skull!"

But it was yet another one of Paws's **gags**.

"**I CAN'T TAKE IT ANYMORE!**" I yelped in exasperation. "Hercule, for the love of all that's cheesy and delicious, we need to get serious if we want to solve the case of the ghost at the *GRAND HOTEL*!"

Paws stopped giggling at once. "A

GHOST at the Grand Hotel? I'm sorry to hear that it's in trouble. It is one of the *finest* establishments in New Mouse City. Tell me what I can do to help."

Hercule perked up his ears and began interrogating him. "We need some **information**, if you please! Has a mouse come in recently and purchased any of the following?"

1. **Glow-in-the-dark paint**
2. **Fake spiderwebs**
3. **Chocolates**
4. **A white wig**
5. **Fake armor**
6. **Plastic chains**
7. **A violin music recording**

Paws checked his records **carefully**. "Yes, there was a rodent who came in here and bought almost all those things — everything except for the chocolates. This is a joke store, not a *sweets shop*!"

"Describe this mouse for me. Was he very very tall or very very **short**? Very very fat or very very THIN?" Hercule asked.

Paws stroked his snout thoughtfully. "He was **SHORT**, and quite thin. He was wearing a **light gray** suit — no, actually it was **black** and PIN-STRIPED. His shirt was a loud color — I think it was **yellow** — and his tie was *embroidered* with the letters **B.B.** He was

a very flashy mouse and he was covered with jewelry. He had **gold** buttons on his jacket and a DIAMOND ring as big as a ball of mozzarella. His shoes were also really **shiny**, and he kept chewing on chocolates. When he left, I had to sweep up a bunch of empty **wrappers** off the floor."

Hercule was perplexed. "There's just one small fly in the fondue. Our trickster ghost is **BIG** and **TALL**, but this rodent is short and thin."

I nodded. "Paws, any idea how we could find the rodent who came in here?"

"I saw him head toward the **HARBOR** in a fancy **stretch limousine**," Paws replied.

We thanked Paws for his help and scurried out of the store.

ONLY THE FINEST FOR OUR B.B.!

As soon as we left the store, we climbed onto the **bananacycle** (Hercule's motorcycle) and zoomed off toward the harbor. We circled around for a while, but our patience **paid off**: We spotted a **huge**, *flashy* limousine as long as a bus. There was no mistaking it! Everything was made of solid gold, even the tires. It shone in the sun like a sweaty slice of Swiss.

Hercule slid on a pair of dark sunglasses. "That thing's so bright I need to wear shades!"

The driver — a rodent as **tall** as a door, as **wide** as a wardrobe, and as threatening as a **mountain lion** — climbed out of the limo, leaving the door open behind him.

"I have a **GENIUS IDEA**. I will investigate the limo!" Hercule declared.

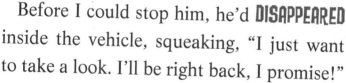

"Stop it, Poirat! Are you crazy?" I cried.

Before I could stop him, he'd **DISAPPEARED** inside the vehicle, squeaking, "I just want to take a look. I'll be right back, I promise!"

I followed him with a sigh. The inside of the limousine was even more **EXTRAORDINARY** than the outside. The steering wheel was **SOLID GOLD**, with the initials **B.B.** engraved in the center. Behind the front seat was a large area

that held little YELLOW COUCHES. The initials B.B. were embroidered on everything!

Hercule spotted a control panel and murmured, "I wonder what all these buttons are for."

"No! Hercule! Don't *touch* those!"

But it was too late — he had already pressed one of the buttons. With a loud buzz, a big cabinet slid open. Inside were an enormouse television and a stereo so big it looked like it belonged in a DANCE CLUB.

Hercule pressed another button, and a GOLDEN HOT TUB in the shape of a B appeared. It had a solid-gold faucet.

He pressed another button, and a B-shaped **bed** slid down. Another button opened a CLOSET in the shape of a

B. It was filled with designer suits, ties, and hats.

Finally, Hercule put his paw on a button that opened a B-shaped **REFRIGERATOR**. It was fully stocked with the finest cheeses!

Hercule immediately began **RUMMAGING** through the refrigerator. "Wow, triple-cheese chocolates and aged **cheddar** — only the finest for our **B.B.**!"

Suddenly, I realized that someone was **coming**. I immediately recognized the approaching mouse from Paws's description. It was him. It was **B.B.**!

B.B.'s stretch limo

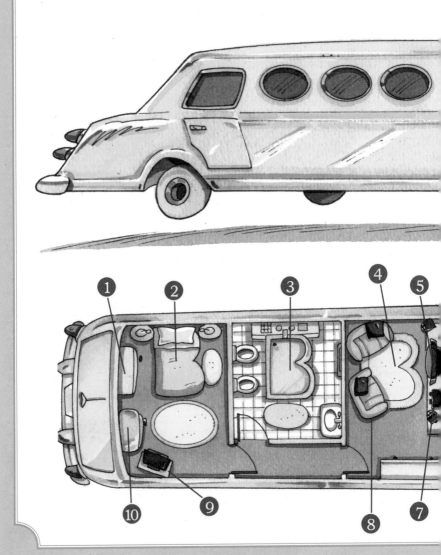

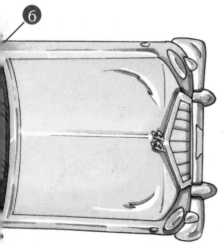

6

1 - CLOSET
2 - BED
3 - HOT TUB
4 - CARPET
5 - GIANT
    TELEVISION
6 - FRONT SEAT
7 - STEREO
8 - COUCHES
9 - SMALLER
    TELEVISION
10 - REFRIGERATOR

He flung open the front door to the limo and scurried in, followed by his driver. Meanwhile, Hercule and I were HIDING right behind them in the backseat! We grabbed each other's paws and held on for dear life as the limo's **engine** started. We were moving!

B.B. pulled a golden cell phone out of his pocket and started to make a **PHONE CALL**.

"Hello? It's me. I have good news for you, Sleezer!"

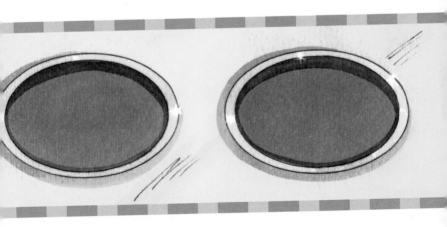

Hearing that name sent chills down my tail. Do you remember Sleezer? That good-for-nothing sewer rat is always trying to take over New Mouse City!

I wanted to hear more of B.B.'s phone call, but unfortunately, the **gigantic limo** stopped and **B.B.** got out, followed by his driver.

Hercule and I waited until the coast was clear. Then we climbed out, too. That was when we realized that we were right in front of *New Mouse City's Grand Hotel*!

B.B. Stands for . . . Bradley Bigbottom!

B.B. strode into the Grand Hotel like he owned the place. Only then did I get a good look at him. He was wearing a BLACK PIN-STRIPED suit with golden buttons, with a WHITE-and-yellow silk shirt underneath, and a flashy tie with the initials B.B. on it. On one paw he had a DIAMOND ring the size of a Cheesy Chew. His orange shoes were very shiny, as if someone had waxed them with butter. He was wearing **dark sunglasses** and a large-brimmed hat. His whiskers glistened with fur-wax. He was surrounded by a cloud of cologne that was stinkier than blue cheese.

B.B. was picking his teeth with an ivory TOOTHPICK. He withdrew it and said to Horatzio, "So? Have you decided to SELL?"

I took a step forward. "My name is Stilton, *Geronimo Stilton*," I said. "I haven't yet had the pleasure of meeting you, sir, but there is something that I would like to say to you. Not everything has a price tag. You can't buy **LOVE**, friendship, freedom, or **peace**. The best things in life are priceless! And among the many things that **cannot** be bought are the history and tradition of Mouse Island and its long-

standing institutions. New Mouse City's *GRAND HOTEL* is not for sale!"

B.B. leaned in close, until our WHISKERS

touched. We stared at each other **snout-to-snout**. Finally, he burst out, "I know who you are! You are the editor of *The Rodent's Gazette*! How much do you want for your newspaper? How much would it cost to take it off your **PAWS**?"

I stared him down. "Sir, you can add *The Rodent's Gazette* to the list of things that you cannot buy!"

"Is that so, **Mr. Big-Shot Editor Mouse**? Yours truly can and will buy whatever I like!" he hissed. "And I'll do it, or my name isn't **Bradley Bigbottom**!"

Then he left.

At that moment, Horatzio came running up. His fur was as white as a bowl of milk. "The ghost is coming! Run! **HEEEELLLLLLLP**!"

A GHOST TRAP!

The ghost **HOWLED**, "*Get ooouuuuut of heeeere, all of yooouuuuu! Thiiiiis iiis myyy hotelllllllll!*"

But the GHOST didn't get far. Hercule and I scurried right up to him and ripped the helmet and wig off his head. Underneath we saw . . . Ms. Bertha!

Only then did some of the strange particulars of the case come back to me. **First of all**, Bertha looked a lot like Bradley Bigbottom. Although she was tall and stout and he was short and thin, she had the same expensive tastes as he did . . . and she also wore the initials **B.B.**!

Then I understood. She was actually Bertha Bigbottom, Bradley Bigbottom's *sister*!

Bertha Bigbottom

Who she is: A very tall and very stout lady mouse who is always dressed elegantly. She is clever and quite snooty.

What she does: She is quite a capable manager. What does she specialize in managing? Anything — as long as she's in charge!

Her plan: She and her brother, Bradley, are in cahoots with Sleezer, a wicked rodent who wants to take over Mouse Island. In exchange for helping, Bertha wants to become president of Mouse Island.

Her secret: She longs to conquer Sleezer's heart.

Her dream: To become the most powerful rodent on Mouse Island!

Her weakness: She is a very greedy mouse.

Bradley Bigbottom

Who he is: A very short and very thin mouse. Like his sister, he is clever and always elegantly dressed.

What he does: He is a shady trader at New Mouse City's harbor. What does he trade? Anything — as long as he can take a big cut!

His plan: He is Sleezer's right-paw mouse. He wants to help him take over Mouse Island. His price: all the gold in all the banks on the island.

His secret: He is a master of special effects.

His dream: To become the richest rodent on Mouse Island!

His weakness: He can't resist cheddar-flavored chocolates.

WHAT A KLUTZ!

"**Bravo!** You rodents are heroes for solving this mystery!" Horatzio exclaimed.

"I'll tell you who the real hero is," Hercule exclaimed. "My dear friend Geronimo Stilton!" He reached over to hug me but accidentally stuck his finger in my eye.

"*Oooouuuuuuuuuchhhhh!*" I squeaked.

"Uh-oh, did I hurt your eye? I'm so sorry!" Hercule **shouted**.

He took me by the paw and led me to the revolving door . . . which my tail got caught in!

"*Oooouuuuuuuuuchhhhh!*" I screeched.

Hercule brought me an **ice cube** for my hurt tail, but he dropped it. I still couldn't see because of my swollen eye, and I slipped on it! · · · · ·

"*Yeee-oouuuuuuuuuchhhhh!* I've broken my leeeeeeeeeeggg!" I cried. "Call 9-1-1!"

Luckily, someone had heard my request, and an **ambulance** soon arrived. I winced in pain as the doctor checked me out. "Yes, sir, it seems that you have broken your leg."

THAT HERCULE POIRAT! WHAT A KLUTZ!

WATCH OUT FOR
THE CAAAAST!

At the **hospital**, they put a cast on my leg. Then they sent me home.

The next day, Hercule Poirat paid me a visit. I could tell he was feeling guilty.

"My dear Stilton, I hope you're **SURVIVING**," he said anxiously. He pawed me a box of banana-flavored **chocolates**. Ugh, I detest bananas. Then he tripped . . . and grabbed my leg to keep from falling!

"*Ooowwwww!*" I yelled. "Watch out for the caaaast!"

"**SORRY SORRY SORRY**, Stilton!" he cried. Then he repositioned my leg on a pawstool and took out a pen. "I'll sign it!"

As he bent over, **he slipped** and smashed

his snout into the cast.

"*Oooowwwwwww!*" I yelled. "Watch out for the caaaast!"

Hercule sprang to his paws again. "**SORRY SORRY SORRY**, my dear Stilton!" Then he opened up the box of **chocolates**. "*Yum-yum-diddly-dum!*" he EXCLAIMED with satisfaction. He began shoveling chocolates into his snout. He was eating so ferociously, he **knocked over** the table . . . which hit me in the leg.

"*Ooowwwww!*" I yelled. "Watch out for the caaaast!"

Hercule scrambled back to his paws. "**SORRY SORRY SORRY**, my dear Stilton!"

I propped myself up on a crutch so I could see him to the door.

At that moment my sister, Thea, arrived . . . **on her motorcycle**! "Howdy, big brother! Aren't you *happy* to see me?"

As she squeaked, she ran into my leg with one of the motorcycle's **TIRES**.

"*Ooowwwww!*" I yelled. "Watch out for the caaaast!"

I sank back down into my pawchair.

Just then my cousin Trap arrived. He gave me a big, hearty SLAP on my cast. "So, it's really broken, huh? You're not faking it?"

"*Ooowwwww!*" I yelled. "Watch out for the caaaast!"

Then my grandfather William Shortpaws showed up. "Geronimo, where did you break the bone? Here or here?" he asked, tapping my leg energetically. "Squeak up, Grandson!"

"*Ooowwwww!*" I yelled. "Watch out for the caaaast!"

Next my friend Creepella strolled in, along with her pet bat, **BITEWING**, who immediately dove for my leg.

"*Ooowwwww!*" I yelled. "Watch out for the caaaast!"

Then came Bruce Hyena, shouting, "Ready for a little PHYSICAL THERAPY, champ? I'll get you back in shape in no time! I'll have you exercising **day** and NIGHT!" He did push-ups on one paw, then lost his **BALANCE** and hit my leg.

"*Ooowwwww!*" I yelled. "Watch out for the caaaast!"

Finally, my editorial assistant, Pinky Pick, came **SKIPPING** in with a radio playing at **full blast**. "Boss, feel like dancing?" she cried exuberantly. She pulled me up and I tried hobbling around on my **crutch**, but then she stepped on my paw.

"*Ooowwwww!*" I yelled. "Watch out for the caaaast!"

I *fell* back into my pawchair just as my nephew Benjamin came in. He took one look at the **CROWD** and cried, "Stop it, everyone! Let Uncle Geronimo **rest**!"

I hugged him gratefully.

"THANK YOU, BENJAMIN. YOU'RE THE ONLY ONE WHO UNDERSTANDS ME!"

GUESS WHO THE GUEST OF HONOR IS!

Horatzio came in just as Benjamin was trying to usher everyone out. "Geronimo, my old friend! Now that you and Hercule have unmasked the ghost, I would like to invite all of New Mouse City to the Grand Hotel tonight for a **GREAT MASQUERADE BALL**! Guess who the **guest of honor** is!"

"I—I—I don't know," I stuttered.

"Why, it's **YOU**, Geronimo Stilton! Who else could it be?" Horatzio cried.

I stammered, "B-but I can't possibly attend, my leg is in a cast. . . ."

"I have a **GENIUS IDEA**!" Hercule exclaimed. "You can dress up as a mummy! The bandages will go perfectly with your cast."

"Quite right, Mr. Poirat!" CRIED Grandfather William. "That is a GENIUS IDEA!"

"I could do with **a little less genius** around here," I muttered. But no one paid any attention to me. The next thing I knew, Hercule had wrapped me in bandages from snout to paw. Just like a **MUMMY**!

So I was forced to attend the **GREAT MASQUERADE BALL**. The whole city was there, in the *GRAND HOTEL'S* ballroom.

As everyone was dancing the *Swiss*

Cheese Shuffle, I looked out the window. The moon was SHINING in the sky, illuminating the rooftops of my sweet New Mouse City.

Oh, how I loved this town!

There were so many **familiar** places: the station, the theater, the library, and the art mouseum. I could also see the cheese market, Singing Stone Plaza, and *The Rodent's Gazette* offices, and all the way on the horizon was the airport.

I felt tied to **ALL** the rodents who lived here, as if our lives were connected by string cheese!

This adventure had truly reminded me that there are things that just **CANNOT** be bought, like the memories, events, and traditions at NEW MOUSE CITY'S GRAND HOTEL. It's a place I'll carry in my heart forever!

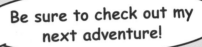

Be sure to check out my next adventure!

THE ENORMOUSE PEARL HEIST

One day, my friends and I, Geronimo Stilton, discovered a huge clam—with an enormouse pearl inside! I was so excited I wrote a special feature about it in *The Rodent's Gazette*. That article attracted lots of attention—both good and bad! The enormouse pearl was in danger of being stolen. Would my friends and I be able to protect it?

#1 Lost Treasure of the Emerald Eye

#2 The Curse of the Cheese Pyramid

#3 Cat and Mouse in a Haunted House

#4 I'm Too Fond of My Fur!

#5 Four Mice Deep in the Jungle

#6 Paws Off, Cheddarface!

#7 Red Pizzas for a Blue Count

#8 Attack of the Bandit Cats

#9 A Fabumouse Vacation for Geronimo

#10 All Because of a Cup of Coffee

#11 It's Halloween, You 'Fraidy Mouse!

#12 Merry Christmas, Geronimo!

#13 The Phantom of the Subway

#14 The Temple of the Ruby of Fire

#15 The Mona Mousa Code

#16 A Cheese-Colored Camper

#17 Watch Your Whiskers, Stilton!

#18 Shipwreck on the Pirate Islands

#19 My Name Is Stilton, Geronimo Stilton

#20 Surf's Up, Geronimo!

#21 The Wild, Wild West

#22 The Secret of Cacklefur Castle

A Christmas Tal

#23 Valentine's Day Disaster

#24 Field Trip to Niagara Falls

#25 The Search for Sunken Treasure

#26 The Mummy with No Name

#27 The Christmas Toy Factory

#28 Wedding Crasher

#29 Down and Out Down Under

#30 The Mouse Island Marathon

#31 The Mysterious Cheese Thief

Christmas Catastrophe

#32 Valley of the Giant Skeletons

#33 Geronimo and the Gold Medal Mystery

#34 Geronimo Stilton, Secret Agent

#35 A Very Merry Christmas

#36 Geronimo Valentine

#37 The Race Across America

#38 A Fabumouse School Adventure

#39 Singing Sensation

#40 The Karate Mouse

#41 Mighty Mount Kilimanjaro

#42 The Peculiar Pumpkin Thief

#43 I'm Not a Supermouse!

#44 The Giant Diamond Robbery

#45 Save the White Whale!

#46 The Haunted Castle

#47 Run for the Hills, Geronimo!

#48 The Mystery in Venice

#49 The Way of the Samurai

#50 This Hotel is Haunted!

Don't miss these very special editions!

THE KINGDOM OF FANTASY

THE QUEST FOR PARADISE: THE RETURN TO THE KINGDOM OF FANTASY

THE AMAZING VOYAGE: THE THIRD ADVENTURE IN THE KINGDOM OF FANTASY

Be sure to check out these exciting Thea Sisters adventures!

Thea Stilton and the Dragon's Code

Thea Stilton and the Mountain Of Fire

Thea Stilton and the Ghost of the Shipwreck

Thea Stilton and the Secret City

Thea Stilton and the Mystery in Paris

Thea Stilton and the Cherry Blossom Adventure

Thea Stilton and the Star Castaways

Thea Stilton: Big Trouble in the Big Apple

Thea Stilton and the Ice Treasure

Thea Stilton and the Secret of the Old Castle

Thea Stilton and the Blue Scarab Hunt

Meet
CREEPELLA VON CACKLEFUR

I, *Geronimo Stilton*, have a lot of mouse friends, but none as **spooky** as my friend CREEPELLA VON CACKLEFUR! She is an enchanting and MYSTERIOUS mouse with a pet bat named Bitewing. YIKES! I'm a real 'fraidy mouse, but even I think CREEPELLA and her family are AWFULLY fascinating. I can't wait for you to read all about CREEPELLA in these fa-mouse-ly funny and **spectacularly spooky** tales!

#1 THE THIRTEEN GHOSTS

#2 MEET ME IN HORRORWOOD

#3 GHOST PIRATE TREASURE

#4 RETURN OF THE VAMPIRE

ABOUT THE AUTHOR

 Born in New Mouse City, Mouse Island, **GERONIMO STILTON** is Rattus Emeritus of Mousomorphic Literature and of Neo-Ratonic Comparative Philosophy. For the past twenty years, he has been running *The Rodent's Gazette*, New Mouse City's most widely read daily newspaper.

Stilton was awarded the Ratitzer Prize for his scoops on *The Curse of the Cheese Pyramid* and *The Search for Sunken Treasure*. He has also received the Andersen 2000 Prize for Personality of the Year. One of his bestsellers won the 2002 eBook Award for world's best ratlings' electronic book. His works have been published all over the globe.

In his spare time, Mr. Stilton collects antique cheese rinds and plays golf. But what he most enjoys is telling stories to his nephew Benjamin.

1. Main entrance
2. Printing presses (where the books and newspaper are printed)
3. Accounts department
4. Editorial room (where the editors, illustrators, and designers work)
5. Geronimo Stilton's office
6. Helicopter landing pad

THE RODENT'S GAZETTE

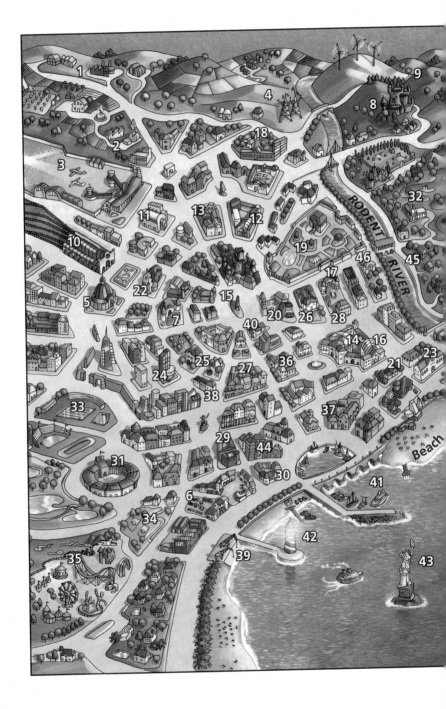

Map of New Mouse City

1. Industrial Zone
2. Cheese Factories
3. Angorat International Airport
4. WRAT Radio and Television Station
5. Cheese Market
6. Fish Market
7. Town Hall
8. Snotnose Castle
9. The Seven Hills of Mouse Island
10. Mouse Central Station
11. Trade Center
12. Movie Theater
13. Gym
14. Catnegie Hall
15. Singing Stone Plaza
16. The Gouda Theater
17. Grand Hotel
18. Mouse General Hospital
19. Botanical Gardens
20. Cheap Junk for Less (Trap's store)
21. Parking Lot
22. Museum of Modern Art
23. University and Library
24. *The Daily Rat*
25. *The Rodent's Gazette*
26. Trap's House
27. Fashion District
28. The Mouse House Restaurant
29. Environmental Protection Center
30. Harbor Office
31. Mousidon Square Garden
32. Golf Course
33. Swimming Pool
34. Blushing Meadow Tennis Courts
35. Curlyfur Island Amusement Park
36. Geronimo's House
37. Historic District
38. Public Library
39. Shipyard
40. Thea's House
41. New Mouse Harbor
42. Luna Lighthouse
43. The Statue of Liberty
44. Hercule Poirat's Office
45. Petunia Pretty Paws's House
46. Grandfather William's House

Brigand's Isle

Tomcat Island

Pirate Ship of Cats

This way to the Rodent Straits

Hamster Islands

Blue Dolphin Bay

Coral Reefs

This way to the Mousific Ocean

Cat's Claw Bay

Panther Archipelago

Swissville

Stray Cat Harbor

Cheddarton

Mouseport

This way to the Ratlantic Ocean

San Mouscisco

New Mouse City

Mousefort Beach

Furflung Island

This way to the Sea of Mice

N
W E
S

MOUSE ISLAND

Map of Mouse Island

1. Big Ice Lake
2. Frozen Fur Peak
3. Slipperyslopes Glacier
4. Coldcreeps Peak
5. Ratzikistan
6. Transratania
7. Mount Vamp
8. Roastedrat Volcano
9. Brimstone Lake
10. Poopedcat Pass
11. Stinko Peak
12. Dark Forest
13. Vain Vampires Valley
14. Goose Bumps Gorge
15. The Shadow Line Pass
16. Penny Pincher Castle
17. Nature Reserve Park
18. Las Ratayas Marinas
19. Fossil Forest
20. Lake Lake
21. Lake Lakelake
22. Lake Lakelakelake
23. Cheddar Crag
24. Cannycat Castle
25. Valley of the Giant Sequoia
26. Cheddar Springs
27. Sulfurous Swamp
28. Old Reliable Geyser
29. Vole Vale
30. Ravingrat Ravine
31. Gnat Marshes
32. Munster Highlands
33. Mousehara Desert
34. Oasis of the Sweaty Camel
35. Cabbagehead Hill
36. Rattytrap Jungle
37. Rio Mosquito

...ouse friends,
Thanks for reading, and farewell
till the next book.
It'll be another whisker-licking-good
adventure, and that's a promise!

Geronimo Stilton